Praise for Storyshares

"One of the brightest innovators and game-changers in the education industry."
— Forbes

"Your success in applying research-validated practices to promote literacy serves as a valuable model for other organizations seeking to create evidence-based literacy programs." — Library of Congress

"We need powerful social and educational innovation, and Storyshares is breaking new ground. The organization addresses critical problems facing our students and teachers. I am excited about the strategies it brings to the collective work of making sure every student has an equal chance in life."
— Teach For America

"It's the perfect idea. There's really nothing like this. I mean, wow, this will be a wonderful experience for young people." — Andrea Davis Pinkney, Executive Director, Scholastic

"Reading for meaning opens opportunities for a lifetime of learning. Providing emerging readers with engaging texts that are designed to offer both challenges and support for each individual will improve their lives for years to come. Storyshares is a wonderful start."
— David Rose, Co-founder of CAST & UDL

Storyshares presents

Published by Storyshares, LLC
Inspiring reading with a new kind of book.

Storyshares
Storyshares, LLC
24 N. Bryn Mawr Avenue #340
Bryn Mawr, Pennsylvania 19010-3304
www.storyshares.org

Interest Level: High School
Grade Level Equivalent: 3.6

ISBN 9798885977708
Book design by Saskia Globig

RACE TO FREEDOM

Tamana Ariq

Storyshares

CONTENTS

ONE

Far From Home

Hot, sweltering, thick air. As dense as honey. It is constantly blistering my lungs. The burning sensation of boiling fingers crawls over my body.

It is only one of our many enemies.

Another is the Taliban.

I was once a young Hazara girl, hopeful of my future, curious of my education. When I had the privilege.

I used to walk freely with my mother through the streets of Kabul, swinging on her arm. We even sometimes shopped at the market.

We didn't need to cover our mouths and noses. We didn't even need to be escorted by a male figure.

Those were the old times. How I long that things would be the same once again.

But I know it can't be. Not for long, anyway.

Because slowly, a terrorist group was rising to new levels. Soon it would take over all of Afghanistan.

They were coming. I knew it. We all knew it. The fear had been clinging to the air, ever since the first cities in the outskirts had been invaded and the Taliban had taken control. And stealthily, like wild cats hunting their dinners, they attacked the cities. One by one, they fell like dominoes.

It was inevitable that we would be next. After all, to seize Kabul meant that the Taliban had risen to power once again.

TWO

My mother shook me awake, that fateful day. Every inch of her face showed fear.

Her eyebrows were creased with anxiety. Her lips a straight line. Her eyes glistening with what seemed like tears.

I knew immediately that the worst had come. I didn't even need her to tell me so.

My eyes were blurry. I could see the hazy, unfocused image of my mother. She was shaking me with one arm. In the other, she held my baby brother defensively. He was only a few days old.

"Hila...." She seemed out of breath. "Hila... they're coming.... we need to go, now."

Maybe that woke me up. I had been dreading this day for years, ever since the Taliban fell.

We all knew that it wasn't the end. That it was the end of a beginning.

And now, they had truly returned to regain "their land."

I bolted upright and swung my feet over the side of my bed. My mother was slightly startled by the sudden movement.

She backed out of the door, telling me she'd be preparing the bags. We didn't have much; I doubted it would take long.

I slipped my feet into my sandals and rushed out.

Outside, my father was cramming the bags into the small car we borrowed from my uncle.

My mother was inside already. She was urging me to hurry.

I didn't even get a second glance at my former home. My father hit the accelerator and we sped along the road.

THREE

I knew that something was seriously wrong.

The streets were quieter, for one thing. Not a single movement.

It didn't seem like there was any living presence. Then we turned onto the main road.

I exhaled. It wasn't what I thought it was.

The main road was busy.

The air was filled with angry, frustrated horns. People honked and pushed.

And we were in the middle of it.

I could tell that they'd had to flee their homes, like we did. They had no other choice. That was the hard truth.

I never thought I would hate anyone more than the Taliban.

Maybe even more than my math teacher.

They are the reason we could never have normal lives. Because we're Hazara, the Taliban believe we don't deserve to have lives. Or to be treated as equals.

Or to live at all.

I don't understand, but then I don't understand many things.

I don't understand math, either.

FOUR

My father honked the horn three times. Many other frustrated drivers that were stuck in the jam honked back.

For some reason, it reminded me of a cluster of furious bees.

We spotted the commotion up ahead. It was two armed soldiers.

Talibs with bushy beards and long, black, intimidating riflles strapped over their chests. They wore camo jackets and pants. And big, black boots.

I saw one of them look inside a car. The other trained his rifle on the passengers inside, in case they dared to do anything.

Which they wouldn't.

I shut my eyes before it happened.

I heard the deafening sound of a gunshot. And then nothing.

The only thing filling the air was the stifled sobs of a distraught mother.

I shuddered. I might be next.

And I knew my father was thinking along that same line of thought.

A chill hung in the air. The atmosphere in the car became tense. Then it was all chaos.

FIVE

People came to their senses, just a few seconds after the gunshot. The screeching of cars reversing and crashing filled the air. People tried desperately to scramble away from the scene.

My father hit the reverse. Our car crashed into a car only an inch behind us.

The driver yelled at us. My father didn't pay any attention.

The two Talibs looked up from the next car they were "inspecting." They raised their guns.

For a second, even though I was sitting in the back seat, we locked eyes. I wished I could just sink into the ground. Except I couldn't. They aimed and fired.

I didn't know which car the shots went into.
I closed my eyes at the last second.

I can only imagine the gore, and the blood, and the screams.

It brings bad memories of when my grandfather died. I didn't understand anything at the time.
I even foolishly believed that he was whisked away to London. That he was receiving the best care.

That's the story my mother told me.

But when I overheard my parents that night,
I knew that my mother only wanted to protect me from the truth.

I found out anyway.

Sometimes, I feel like despite all my flaws and my shameful grades, people underestimate me.

My father furiously turned the steering wheel.
The car spun around. He hit the accelerator. We sped away into an alleyway and out of sight.

SIX

A Portal to Another World

I never thought I'd see anywhere outside my home again. The Taliban said that women shouldn't go to school. They said we had to be escorted by a male figure outside.

I never thought that my family would have to flee our homes to save our lives. But that was before the Taliban existed.

So, there we were, doing just that. And it broke my heart.

I could tell that my father didn't care about where we were going as much as he cared about putting distance between us and the Talibs.

We knew then what was at stake. The Talibs

were already closing in on us fast.

We had to be faster if we were to get out of this alive.

I clutched the edge of my seat for dear life as we twisted and turned. I was thrown back and forth and sideways as we jolted around sharp turns in our small, bouncy car.

I'm honestly surprised we even got that far.

But it turned out I was wrong, as usual.

SEVEN

My father did know where he was going.

I didn't know when I fell into a trance-like state, but I bolted awake. The car had stopped with a jerk.

My parents dove outside with my baby brother. I followed them.

I gave my father a puzzled look. "Where are we?"

"Not now, Hila Jan," my father told me.

Jan means "my dear." I was always his dear. He'll always be my loving father.

I nodded.

My father slammed the door shut, but didn't bother to lock it. That frightened me.

I wondered if it would be the last time we saw our car, too.

We each had a small backpack strapped on our backs. They carried a few clothes and essentials. A tiny bit of food.

No possessions, though. There was no space for them. They had to be left behind.

Despite how much I hated my math books, I would have given anything to have them with me right then.

We walked the rest of the journey. No one said a word as we did. Not even my baby brother—Akram—who was often very bubbly.

Eventually, we reached high land. I looked at the sight below. I don't know what I expected.

Below us was the ugliest place. A murky, dirty swamp. It was frothing with dirtiness, like some witch's cauldron.

And there was more to it. In my horror, I couldn't see or think clearly.

Was it.... No, I must be dreaming.... It can't be humans?

But it was.

I pinched myself, but the scene was as vivid as could be.

People were standing in the middle of it. People were standing in the swamp. They were stand-

ing with their clusters of families, a tingle of hope
in their expressions.

I have never seen something so wrong.

EIGHT

The refugees all seemed scruffy, dirty, and exhausted.

Was this filthy passage truly our gate to freedom? Was it the last obstacle to the Western world?

When we were allowed to watch TV, I remember watching cartoons about cities like London. The cartoons showed London as a free city.

Women and men were equal, with the same opportunities. Women were free to wear any type of clothing without so much as a disapproving look.

Everyone, no matter where they were from, was treated with fairness. Even if you were Hazara.

My father spoke a lot about London. Most of it sounded like a dream. Even he doubted the dream would ever come true.

He used to work as an interpreter for British officials, before the Talib took power. His job became too risky.

My eyes always widened when he talked about London. That was heaven on earth, surely.

But when I scanned my eyes over the devastating swamp, crawling with disease and dirt, that dream didn't seem as real as I thought it was.

NINE

It was only when my father was a few feet down the steep hill that I realized he really meant it.

We were going down there.

With the other refugees.

My mother beckoned me to follow, waving to me with her free hand. She clutched Akram and almost slipped. Would have, if my father hadn't caught her.

I took a deep breath. I began the journey downward.

Once or twice, I stumbled. My father's reassuring arm lashed out and grabbed me tightly. All I wanted to do was to be swallowed in his embrace.

With much difficulty, we somehow made it down. We got a few scratches and bruises, but nothing worse.

Hell on earth. That was all that I could think.

We cautiously made our way through the waist-height swamp water. I tried not to look at people while we passed.

I didn't succeed.

The first couple I passed looked terrible. One was an elderly woman, perhaps a grandmother. She was accompanied by a woman and a husband.

The old woman's face was scattered with wrinkles. Her hair was gray.

She was leaning against the wall. Feeble. Weak.

She breathed heavily through her mouth. Her chest heaved with each breath. The woman and the man huddled close.

I looked away. I couldn't bear to watch anymore.

TEN

From what I saw, I got an idea of the state the other refugees were in.

Women in burqas, their eyes reflecting their fear and distress.

Men trying to support their families, but knowing they had little ability to help them.

The twisted, painful faces. Children robbed of their childhood and their lives.

I could almost see the souls of the refugees drained out of them. I refused to take in anymore. It was more crowded than it looked from on top of the hill. We moved through the crowd of people, careful not to so much as brush someone.

I grasped my father's hand as if my life depended on it.

I just couldn't figure it out. What had we Hazaras done to deserve this fate? Why did our kind have to be persecuted and hunted down like animals?

Why couldn't it just be?

ELEVEN

Afghanistan used to be a place where people of all races and kinds were welcomed. Before the Talibs rose to power. Hazaras, Pashtuns, whatever ethnic group, it didn't matter. They were all welcome.

Or so my grandfather told me.

There was peace. People couldn't have been any happier.

We had a decent leader, and the country stood firm while he ruled. President Mohammed Najibul-lah Ahmadzai was abducted by the Taliban merely for being a decent leader.

And they preach Islam.

My father always tells me that if religion doesn't

make you a good person, then you would be better off not having a religion.

We are Muslims, too, but the Taliban are
extremists.

My father is the only literate person in the
family. He is convinced the Taliban's teachings are
wrong, according to the Holy Quran.

TWELVE

I wasn't aware that I was sinking my nails into my father's palms. He looked down at me, gave me a reassuring squeeze, and forced a smile.

I love him.

I tried to think of that Afghanistan my grandfather told me about. If it was just a story or actually true, I don't know.

Still, the Afghanistan where I was as free as a bird and we could all live in peace sparked a flurry of hope in me. That spark kept me going.

The warm thoughts blinded me to my true reality. My senses went numb as my father guided me.

Something collided with my side. I looked down

and let out a scream.

A woman with her hands on her stomach, her eyes closed. She had an equally lifeless baby strapped on her chest.

She seemed at peace, but I was shaken to my core. That could have been my mother.

She's asleep, I thought.

But I was smart enough to know that she wasn't.

In such horrible conditions, with no toilet areas or good places to sleep, disease spread like wildfire. I suppose the woman caught a deadly illness.

My father lowered himself, so he was level with me. I knew by the brisk pace he was going that he was in a hurry.

His eyes were calm, like they always were. But this time I wasn't reassured.

"Hila.... you must trust me."

I nodded.

We continued our daunting, endless journey forward.

THIRTEEN

Out of nowhere, all of a sudden, a riot broke out. It was so unexpected, I was shocked into stillness.

Up ahead were the British army officials. Some were supposed to maintain the peace. Others were supposed to scan the documents that were being waved in the air.

But now, they were all waving their rifles. They were trying to get back some control. Establish authority once again.

I watched in horror as people launched themselves at the soldiers. Some grabbed for the rifles.

That's when the gunshots echoed into the sky. I instinctively thrust my arms over my head. Then, I felt a yank on my arm.

A hand was reaching up from the water and seized my arm. It was like something out of a horror movie.

"Help!" I tried to scream.

I was being dragged into the swamp.

My knees gave way. I collapsed into the swamp.

FOURTEEN

Darkness, only darkness. The murkiness of the swamp. I barely saw any light above me.

I still heard the muffled sounds of shouts and yells and chaos, but I was distant.

I was drowning and I knew it. I felt the ache in my lungs as my brain slowly began to shut down.

I was going to die. Maybe heaven would be better, much better. I wouldn't have to suffer the pain of being a Hazara, for one thing.

Maybe this was the gate to freedom. Maybe I had to die.

And then I would meet more of my kind and be reunited with them. Happily ever after.

Except it wasn't like that.

FIFTEEN

Just then, a hand swooped down on me and grabbed my arm. It yanked me out of the swamp.

I gasped as I exhaled and quickly inhaled deep breaths of air.

Swamp water was streaming down my face. It mixed with sweat and dirt. But I was alive. And thank God.

My father embraced me tightly. My mother offered me a smile. I returned it, but I think it turned out to be more of a grimace. I could tell she was in pain, too.

SIXTEEN

We continued our journey until we reached the officers at the small island with their Jeep trucks.

I watched a pack of refugees whisked away in one of them. This was our ticket to freedom. To the Western world and a diverse place that would welcome us.

My father confidently walked up to one of the soldiers. This one had short hair, a bristly, short beard, and muscular arms.

His eyes were stern, but familiar. Like he had seen too much to ever forget.

That look is too familiar in Afghanistan.

My father spoke in English. Even though I

wasn't an expert, I got an idea of what he was saying.

He was holding the documents and showing them to the soldier. The soldier ran his eyes over them, but didn't say a word.

After my father finished speaking, the soldier finally spoke up. I trained my eyes on him and noticed his every muscle twitch as he spoke.

I should've known by my father's disappointed look that it was gone.

There was no hope.

No hope for a future where we could be welcomed and free. No hope to live in a peaceful society, flourishing with diverse cultures.

I asked him anyway.

SEVENTEEN

He gave me a sad look and explained, "He says our documents are invalid."

I frowned.

My father turned back to the soldiers. He seemed to be arguing. It appeared to be a very tense quarrel.

I caught a name. Both the soldier and my father repeated it several times.

Abdulllah. Abdullah. Abdullah.

He was somehow related to my father's interpreting job.

My father faced me again and translated in Farsi.

"I asked them to call Abdullah, but they say there's no such person in their department. He sent me this letter and told me he will meet me here."

My father tried one last time to try and change the soldier's mind. The attempt had no effect on the soldier.

Then a man appeared.

I'd never seen Abdullah. I didn't know him.

But I knew immediately this was the man we were after.

He looked genuinely confused and curious. I thought he asked what the matter was.

He locked eyes with my father. My father let out an exclamation of relief. Even I knew that was what it was.

Me, not knowing any English.

They shook hands. Then my father, broken by relief, embraced Abdullah.

The man with the bushy beard and warm eyes was stunned for a moment. Then he embraced him back.

EIGHTEEN

They guided us into a truck. The Jeep trucks.

We were crammed in with other refugees. Some I noticed were children, alone. Others were men and teenagers. Not many women. But we were alive. That was what mattered.

I could have died a number of painful ways that day, but God spared me.

I can't forget that.

As the Jeep started, I couldn't help but think about my future.

A future where Hazaras and everyone else could live unchallenged.

A future where I would be living like in the cartoons I watched.

A future where Akram and I could grow up. Be educated and employed, and honor our family.

About the Author

Meet Tamana Ariq, born and raised in London, a 14-year-old prodigy in the realms of poetry, creative writing, and writing novels herself. She wields words as both a canvas and a voice, shedding light on pressing issues, with a special focus on the often-overlooked Afghanistan, as well as specialising in the world of fantasy, and soon, will hopefully publish in the genre of sci-fi. Inspired through natural landscapes and the COVID lockdowns, she published her first ever book in 2021 on Amazon, *The Destiny*, the first book in *The Master Chronicles*. She has already left her mark in the literary world, winning prestigious competitions like the Young Writers and Sweet Education contests and also an active contributor to the esteemed BMT Proud to Be organisation. But her true passion lies in inspiring the next generation, by encouraging young minds to embrace the magic of creative writing guiding them on journeys to far-off lands and uncharted adventures. Through her pen, she showcases the extraordinary impact of creativity in the world of fiction, regardless of age. Join her on this journey through fantastical lands and imaginative tales, where words hold the magic to change the world.

About the Publisher

Storyshares is a publisher focused on supporting the millions of teens and adults who struggle with reading by creating a new shelf in the library specifically for them. The ever-growing collection features content that is compelling and culturally relevant for teens and adults, yet still readable at a range of lower reading levels.

Storyshares generates content by engaging deeply with writers, bringing together a community to create this new kind of book. With more intriguing and approachable stories to choose from, the teens and adults who have fallen behind are improving their skills and beginning to discover the joy of reading.

For more information, visit storyshares.org.

Easy to Read. Hard to Put Down.